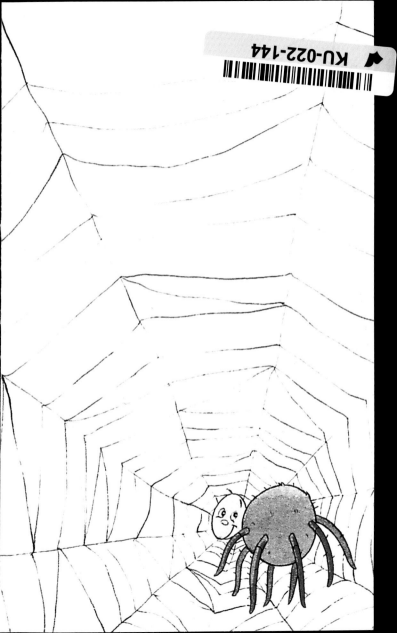

The Musicians of Bremen

Retold by Judy Hamilton
Illustrated by R. James Binnie

Tarantula Books

In a small village, a few miles outside a town called Bremen, there was once an old donkey. He had worked hard for the same master all his life without complaint. Now that old age was upon him, he was no longer strong enough to carry the same heavy loads or walk the same miles. He deserved a happy retirement, but he knew that his master was going to have him killed, so one day he broke his tethering rope and and slipped away.

"All my life I have done as my master wished. Now is the time for me to do as *I* wish. I am going to Bremen to become a musician," he said.

The donkey had not travelled far, when he saw an old dog puffing and panting by the roadside.

The donkey stopped beside the dog and nuzzled him in a friendly way.

"You look tired, old chap. Have you far to go?"

The dog sighed. "I don't know. I ran away from my master today. He was planning to shoot me because I'm too old to hunt."

"Your story is very like mine," nodded the donkey. "I've run away as well, to escape the slaughterhouse. I am going to Bremen to become a musician. Why don't you come too?"

The dog was pleased to find a friend, and agreed. So the two animals set off together.

Turning a corner in the road, they found a cat sitting in the middle of the road, wearily cleaning itself.

The cat had another sorry tale to tell.

"I used to hunt mice for the farmer," it told them, "but I'm too slow to catch them now. The farmer said I would have to be drowned. I had to leave as quickly as I could."

"All cats can sing," said the dog, "I listen to them sometimes at night. Why don't you come and sing with our band? We're going to make our living as musicians in Bremen."

"What a good idea," said the cat, "I was afraid that would starve!"

The donkey, the dog and the cat walked down the road together, full of plans. Then, perched on a wall by the road, they saw a very sad looking cockerel.

"Nobody likes my singing any more," the cockerel to the three animals. "They were going to wring my neck and boil me in the soup pot!"

The others welcomed the cockerel with his fine voice into their band, and now there were four on the road to Bremen.

It was growing dark. They needed to find somewhere spend the night, so they turned off the road into a small wood.

The cockerel spotted a light through the trees.

"Perhaps there's a house over there," he said. "Why don't we take a look? There may be food there."

The others all cheered up at the thought of food. The c led the way towards the light.

The cockerel was right. Soon the animals came to a cottage in a clearing in the trees. There was a lot of noise and laughter coming from inside. The donkey sidled up to a window and looked in.

"Robbers!" the donkey whispered to his friends. "It looks like they're having a party! There's enough food on the table to feed a hundred people, and, oh! you should see the piles of gold and jewels!"

"I'd like to get inside there," said the dog wistfully.

"Lots of food and a place to stay the night; yes, it would be lovely!" agreed the cockerel. "But how can we get in there?"

"I think I may have the answer to that," said the cat with a wink.

"This is how we will do it....."

Following the cat's instructions, the animals piled themselves one on top of the other; first, the donkey, then the dog, then the cat, with the cockerel perched precariously on top. They wobbled up close to the window, then at the cat's signal, they burst into the loudest song they could sing. The noise was appalling braying, barking, yowling and crowing. The robbers were startled and very frightened. The animals kept up the noise as they smashed their way in through the window.

"AAH! Monsters!" yelled the robbers, sending food and furniture flying in their rush to get out, too frightened to look and see what was really happening. Within seconds, the robbers were gone.

The four animals ate well that night in the cottage. There was plenty of food to suit all tastes, so they ate and ate until they were almost too full to move. Finally, they set about making themselves comfortable for sleep. The donkey wandered into the courtyard where he found a clean, dry pile of straw to lie on. The dog snuggled into a corner behind the front door, an old cushion under his head. The cockerel perched at the end of the mantelpiece. The cat, enjoying the heat from the still warm ashes, settled himself on the rug in front of the fire and curled up tight in a ball of fur.

They were all very tired. It had been a long and exciting day. One by one, they fell asleep.

Meanwhile the robbers were talking in the woods beside the cottage. They had been foolish to run away so fast. They had left all their stolen booty behind.

"We don't even know what it was that frightened us!" said one.

"It might have gone away by now," said another.

"I think one of us should go back and see," said the third.

They all turned to the youngest and smallest robber. "You go!" they ordered.

Nervously, the youngest robber crept through the trees. He tiptoed towards the cottage. He opened the back door and peered into the darkness.

The youngest robber felt his way carefully through the hallway and into the living room. He tried not to make any noise. Suddenly, he tripped over a chair leg, and only just stopped himself from falling. The sound of his stumble disturbed the cat, who opened her eyes. The dog also had woken, but lay silently in his corner by the front door listening.

The robber caught sight of the cat's eyes glowing in the darkness by the fireplace. He thought they were embers still glowing in the ashes of the fire.

"If I light a match on these embers, I will be able to see better," he thought. He felt in his pockets and found a match. Tiptoeing up to the fireplace he stuck the match in the cat's eye . . .

The cat hissed and angrily clawed the robber. As the robber fought to get free, the cockerel flapped past him, his wings beating against the robber's face. The robber screamed in pain and stumbled to the front door. The dog pounced, and sank his teeth deep into the robber's leg. The robber screamed and staggered out of the front door. In the courtyard, the shadowy figure of the donkey was waiting for him. "THUMP!" the donkey gave him an almighty kick. Moaning in pain and trembling with fear, the youngest robber limped back to his comrades.

The cockerel flew up to the cottage roof to bid him farewell; "COCK-A-DOODLE-DOO!" he crowed gleefully "COCK-A-DOODLE-DO-OO!"

The youngest robber told his friends a strange tale.

"The house is full of monsters and evil spirits!" he gasped. "We can never go back there! See my face and arms? A demon witch gouged at me with her talons! When I fought to get free, a winged phantom flew past me and beat me with its wings! Then a black monster plunged a knife into my leg when I tried to escape! Another monster in the yard hit me so hard with two clubs that I was sent flying! And I could hear a voice from on high, calling 'DOOM-WILL-COME-TO-YOU! DOOM-WILL-COME-TO-YOU!'"

After the awful experiences of the youngest robber, none of the robbers dared return to the cottage to collect their stolen booty. And what was more, none of them dared steal again. Every time they felt tempted, the youngest robber reminded them of the voice crying 'DOOM-WILL-COME-TO-YOU!', and they changed their minds. Crime did not pay, they decided.

As for the animals, they decided to settle in the cottage in the woods, and there they spent a long and comfortable retirement. They never did go to Bremen, and they forgot all about becoming musicians, but it did not matter.

They had had a great adventure together and now they had as happy a life as anyone could wish for.

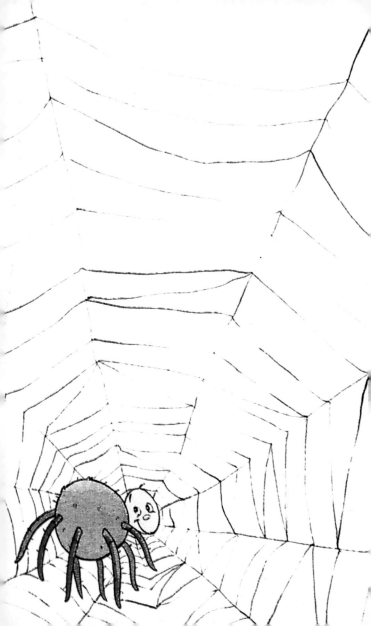